Always My Grandpa

Always My Grandpa

A Story for Children About Alzheimer's Disease

written by Linda Scacco, Ph.D.

illustrated by Nicole Wong

MAGINATION PRESS

WASHINGTON, D.C.

To my husband, Ed, and to
my three children, Katherine,
Molly, and Michael—LS

For Gramma—NW

Published by
MAGINATION PRESS
An Educational Publishing Foundation Book
American Psychological Association
750 First Street, NE
Washington, DC 20002

For more information about our books, including a complete catalog,
please write to us, call 1-800-374-2721, or visit our website at www.maginationpress.com.

Editor: Kristine Enderle
Designer: Michael Hentges
The text type is Monotype Walbaum
Printed by Worzalla, Stevens Point, Wisconsin

Library of Congress Cataloging-in-Publication Data

Scacco, Linda.
Always my grandpa : a story for children about Alzheimer's disease / by Linda Scacco ;
illustrated by Nicole Wong.
     p. cm.
"An Educational Publishing Foundation book."
Summary: During a summer at his grandfather's house, young Daniel, with his mother's help, begins
to understand Alzheimer's disease and how it affects not only Grandpa but the entire family as well.
ISBN 1-59147-311-X (hardcover : alk. paper) ISBN 1-59147-312-8 (pbk. : alk. paper)
[1. Alzheimer's disease—Fiction. 2. Grandfathers—Fiction. 3. Old age—Fiction. 4. Mothers and
sons—Fiction. 5. Storytelling—Fiction.] I. Wong, Nicole E., ill. II. Title.
PZ7.S2759AL 2005
[Fic]—dc22
                                                                                        2005006145

10 9 8 7 6 5 4 3 2 1

Daniel's grandfather is a fisherman
and a storyteller, and he lives
in a house by the sea.

Every summer Daniel and his mother visit him

there. He and Mom pack up the car with bathing

suits, beach towels, baseball gloves, and books.

Then they drive the long and beautiful roads to

Grandpa's house.

They travel on four highways. They cross over seven rivers. Along the way, they search for getting-closer clues. Mom looks for pine needles and soft sand along the edges of the road. Daniel looks for cranberry bogs and kettle ponds and watches the skies for seagulls. Mom rolls down the window to smell the pine trees. Sea air blows wet and salty on her face.

"Mom, I see Grandpa's cottage! We're here!" yells Daniel.

Daniel loves their summer visits. He can't wait to see Grandpa, and he can't wait to see his summer friend Jimmy. Jimmy's cottage is next to Grandpa's, and Jimmy likes baseball just as much as Daniel does.

"Remember, Daniel," says Mom as she pulls the car up to the cottage, "Grandpa will not be the same as when we last saw him."

Daniel hasn't forgotten. Grandpa had been to the doctor in the spring. He had been forgetting things, and a couple of times had gone to the grocery store and couldn't find his way back home. The doctor told Mom that Grandpa had Alzheimer's disease.

"That doesn't sound so bad," Daniel said when Mom first told him. "I forget things too. I forget to hang up my coat sometimes when I come inside from playing."

"This is different, honey," Mom had said quietly. "Grandpa will become more and more forgetful and confused, until one day he won't remember anything, not even us.

"I don't think Grandpa will be any different,"
says Daniel as he grabs his glove and ball, and
hops from the car. "There is no way Grandpa
will ever forget us. I won't let him!"

Daniel pushes open the gate that leads into Grandpa's yard. He runs up the porch stairs two at a time, straight to Grandpa. Daniel wraps his arms around him and so does Mom.

"Grandpa, do you have a story for me? A story about your days and nights on the fishing boat?"

"Let's help your Mom unpack first," says Grandpa, "and then play some catch. I've been waiting all spring and my glove's ready. After we play I'll have lots of stories for you."

Grandpa and Daniel play catch. They toss high-flying pop-ups and pitch fastballs to each other. Grandpa's sneaky curve ball is as good as ever. They play until the sun begins to set.

"Look, Daniel, the sea is wrapping her arms around the sun, like a mother tucking her baby in for the night," says Grandpa in a soft and gentle voice.

Daniel and Grandpa sit on the porch, and
Grandpa tells his stories. Daniel has heard these
stories many times before, but he never gets tired
of them. Everything feels the same, just like
Daniel thought it would.

The next day, Daniel runs off with his glove
and ball to see Jimmy. They play catch and look
at Jimmy's new baseball cards until Mom calls
Daniel home for lunch. Then Mom, Grandpa,
and Daniel spend the afternoon on the beach.
Later Grandpa tells stories.

This summer starts out just like all the other ones Daniel remembers, playing catch with Grandpa and Jimmy, walking along the beach, sitting on the porch listening to Grandpa's stories, and watching the sunset.

But as the days pass, Daniel knows that something has changed.

Mom says Grandpa is having trouble finding all the things that belong to him, his clothes, his words, his memories. Mom says this happens because Grandpa has Alzheimer's disease, and that Grandpa's brain cells are tangled up and dying.

One day Grandpa says to Daniel, "I'm sorry this is happening to me, and to all of us. The doctors tell me that things will get worse over the next few years. Some days will be good, and some days not so good."

"I'm sorry too, Grandpa," says Daniel.

"I want you to know that when I don't seem like myself, or when I'm acting in a way that seems strange or confusing to you, I still love you. I want you to remember that," says Grandpa. "As for today, I feel just like the old fisherman and storyteller I've always been."

Grandpa winks and laughs, and Daniel laughs too.

"Can you tell me a story now, Grandpa?"
Daniel asks.

Grandpa nods and tells Daniel one of his favorite
stories about his greatest fishing catch. Daniel
has heard this funny story many times before,
but he laughs just as loud now as he ever did.

One day something happens that makes Daniel know that things really are changing.

"Let's go look for some shells while Grandpa naps," says Mom. "The tide is low, and we can walk way out to the flats. And I bet the tide pools will be warm too."

"Okay, let's go!" says Daniel. Little fish and fiddler crabs tickle their feet as they walk through the tide pools.

On their way back, Daniel finds a huge seashell. It is sparkly and rough on the outside and soft pinkish on the inside. Mom takes it and looks at it for a long time, carefully turning it over and over in her hands. She lifts it into the air and moves it around very gently.

"Long ago a beautiful creature lived in this seashell, and he danced and danced on the ocean floor," says Mom.

"Let's take it home," Daniel says, "I want to show it to Grandpa."

Daniel is in a hurry to see Grandpa back at the cottage, so he runs ahead. Something smells funny as he throws open the kitchen door. It's a burning smell. Mom rushes in behind him. She knows something is wrong too. Quickly she grabs the burning pan from the stove and takes it outside. She yells at Daniel to open the kitchen window.

"Where are you, Dad?" calls Mom. Her voice sounds mad.

Daniel and Mom find Grandpa in his room. He's sitting at the edge of the bed staring at the floor.

"Dad, you left eggs boiling on the stove," Mom cries. "You could have burned down the whole house!"

Grandpa looks at them. His blue eyes are scared. "Who are you? Get out of my house!" He doesn't seem to know them. Grandpa's hands are shaking, like little birds trying to land in his lap.

Daniel feels really afraid.

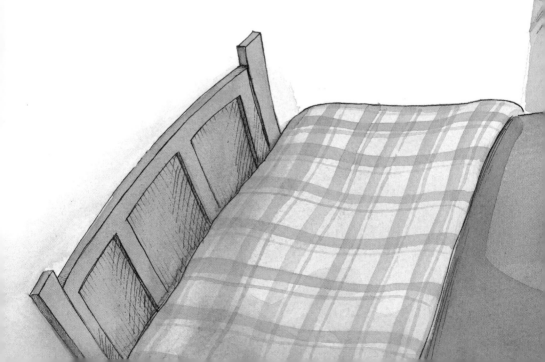

Mom goes over to Grandpa. "I'm sorry, Dad.
It's me, Carol," she says. "It's okay. We're here
with you now."

Daniel watches for a while, then he moves closer.

"It's me, Daniel," he says, touching Grandpa's
shoulder. Grandpa looks at Daniel and takes
Daniel's hand.

That night Mom goes into Daniel's room to say goodnight.

"Mom, you sounded mad at Grandpa today," Daniel says.

"Yes, I guess I was mad," says Mom. "I was so worried about what could have happened. People with Alzheimer's disease become confused and forgetful. Sometimes they do things that aren't safe, like what Grandpa did today. I know he didn't mean to. But I'll have to watch him more carefully."

"I'm scared about what's happening to Grandpa," says Daniel. Daniel is holding the beautiful shell they had found that afternoon.

"I am too, Daniel," says Mom. "You know, Grandpa's mind is like this shell. Once it was full of life and memories. But now, Grandpa's life and memories are leaving him, just like the dancing creature left this shell." She kissed Daniel on the forehead. "Let's get some sleep, and tomorrow we'll show Grandpa your beautiful shell."

At breakfast the next day, Daniel sits quietly
at the table. He doesn't feel like talking much.
He pokes at his cereal and stares out to the sea.

"Are you feeling a little scared about what
happened yesterday?" asks Mom. "Would you
like to talk about it?" Daniel shakes his head and
closes his eyes. Instead the question he's been
thinking about comes out: "Will Grandpa die?"

"Yes, Daniel, he will," says Mom as she reaches
to hold his hand, "and because Grandpa has
Alzheimer's disease, that may happen sooner than
we would expect for a man Grandpa's age."

Daniel is quiet for a moment, then asks,
"Will you and Daddy die too?"

"Not for a very, very long time," says Mom, and
she smiles at Daniel. "Your Daddy and I will be
around to take care of you, and you will be here
with us too."

Daniel feels a little better and not so scared.
"Mom, I'm going to call Jimmy to see if he
wants to come over."

Daniel and Jimmy play catch on the beach while Grandpa watches. Grandpa calls out to Daniel, "Who are you playing with, Daniel?" Daniel is confused. Grandpa has known Jimmy for a long time. "It's Jimmy, from down the road."

Later Grandpa asks again, "Who's the little boy you're playing with, Daniel?"

"It's Jimmy, Grandpa. You know. He lives over there." Not much later Grandpa asks the same question again. Now Daniel shouts, "It's Jimmy, Grandpa, I just told you!"

How could Grandpa forget this after Daniel just told him two times? Jimmy gives Grandpa a funny look and says, "What's wrong with him?"

"Nothing," Daniel says. "Let's go somewhere else and play." They walk farther along the beach to where Grandpa can't see them.

They toss the ball back and forth until Jimmy starts to throw so hard that Daniel misses a few times. Finally Daniel throws down his glove and says, "I don't feel like playing catch with you anymore. You are just showing off!"

"Well, maybe you're just a lousy catcher," says Jimmy.

"I'm going home," Daniel shouts, and he grabs his glove and heads back to the cottage.

Daniel rushes in and slams the door. "What's the matter?" says Mom.

"Jimmy makes me so mad!" Daniel says. "He was throwing balls wild, all over the place."

"It doesn't sound like you're having a great day," says Mom.

"And when Grandpa couldn't remember who Jimmy was," says Daniel, "Jimmy made fun of him!"

"Oh, Daniel, I'm sorry," Mom says. "Some of the things Grandpa does can be embarrassing and hard to explain, especially to other people who don't know about Alzheimer's disease. I know how worried and scared you are. I feel worried too. When we're having these kinds of feelings, sometimes we get mad at people we care about. Remember how I yelled at you for not clearing the table yesterday? And now you're mad at Jimmy. These things happen because we're upset about Grandpa."

Mom pauses and then says, "If you're ever having feelings that upset you, we can talk and I can try to help you figure it out. And maybe tomorrow we can go over to Jimmy's and talk to him and his mom about what's happening to Grandpa. Would you like to do that?" Mom asks.

Daniel nods. "I guess I should say I'm sorry too." Mom smiles.

The summer passes. Some days Grandpa is okay.
Some days they all walk to the library. Some days
Grandpa, Daniel, and Jimmy take walks along
the beach. Some days they stop along the way to
talk to some of Grandpa's friends. Some days
Daniel listens to Grandpa's stories as the sun sets.

But some days Grandpa is confused and hardly talks at all. Sometimes Grandpa sits at the edge of his bed and stares straight ahead like he can't figure out what to do next. Some days he can't find his hat or his shoes or his shirt. Some days he can't find the right words for what he wants to say. Sometimes he is grumpy and gets mad at Mom and Daniel.

"Grandpa gets mad at me for the dumbest things," cries Daniel. "He got mad at me because I put my towel on the wrong hook!"

"Grandpa isn't doing these things on purpose," Mom says. "I think Grandpa just needs things to be in order right now. It helps him keep his memories in the right place. Grandpa loves us. He's just confused about things."

"I know Grandpa loves me," says Daniel. "He's just not the same as he used to be."

"When we leave here at the end of the summer, Grandpa will come home with us," Mom says one day. "We'll take care of him, at least for now. But someday Grandpa will need more care than we'll be able to give him. I'll need to look for a special hospital for him when that time comes."

"Will we come back here next summer with Grandpa?" Daniel asks. "Will this be our last summer with Grandpa in his house by the sea?"

"I hope not," says Mom. "It all depends on how Grandpa is doing."

"I'll miss Grandpa's stories," says Daniel.

Mom nods. "I will too. I've heard Grandpa's stories since I was a little girl. I'll miss them very much." She smiles at Daniel. "But you know Grandpa's stories. You will tell them. You are the storyteller now."

That night as Daniel sleeps, Grandpa's stories fill
his dreams.

When the summer ends, Mom and Daniel say goodbye to Jimmy and pack up the car to head back home. Grandpa sits with Daniel in the back seat. They travel back on four highways and cross over seven rivers. They look for clues that they are getting closer.

Sometimes Grandpa asks, "Where are you taking us, Carol?"

Mom answers the same way every time. "You're coming home with us, Dad."

"Okay, honey, that will be nice," says Grandpa.

Daniel and Grandpa take turns holding the beautiful shell. Daniel tells stories about the creature who once lived inside and who danced on the ocean floor. He tells stories about Grandpa's days and nights on the fishing boat. He tells how the sea wraps her arms around the sun, like a mother tucking her baby in for the night. Grandpa seems to understand. Daniel talks and talks all the way home, and Grandpa listens and nods and smiles.

Note to Parents

CHILDREN CAN EXPERIENCE a variety of feelings when a grandparent or other adult they know has Alzheimer's disease. As confusing symptoms and behaviors emerge in the person, a child may feel sad, worried, embarrassed, or angry. Over time, a child might withdraw from family members or get in fights with friends and siblings. Your child may become stressed and anxious, especially as your family dynamics change. Children do not adjust easily to the ongoing changes that Alzheimer's disease brings. Your child may ask questions like: Why is Grandpa acting this way? Why is he so angry? Why does Grandma ask the same question over and over? Why does she act like a kid? Why can't Grandma take care of this stuff herself? By understanding the psychological issues that confront a young child and explaining the disease in age-appropriate language, parents can greatly reduce their child's distress.

Explain the disease.
Tell your child in words he or she understands that Alzheimer's disease is a brain disorder. People with Alzheimer's will become increasingly confused and unable to carry out activities such as cooking, cleaning, and caring for themselves. Although the exact cause of Alzheimer's is unknown, researchers know that irreversible changes in a person's brain cause brain cells to die. As cells die, normal memory, reasoning, and communication are severely impaired. Also, behavior and personality can drastically change: A person with Alzheimer's disease may become aggressive, anxious, delusional, or depressed.

Describe your role as caregiver.

A person with Alzheimer's typically will live from 8 to 20 years from the onset of symptoms. Frequently much of that time is spent under the vigilant care of a spouse or relative. To prepare your child for this, explain that a considerable amount of time will be dedicated to caring for her grandparent. And to help keep her from feeling displaced or resentful, make sure she feels like an important part of the family. Basic chores and routine tasks like folding clothes or putting away groceries might help your children interact with their grandparent in a comfortable and positive way. Also try to keep the family rules, rituals, and schedules the same.

Help children identify their feelings.

Parents can help children sort through all their sad, angry, or frustrated feelings. Talking about feelings will allow your child to identify them and realize that it's okay to feel that way. You should empathize with your child but also acknowledge when he demonstrates patience and understanding. You might say, "It is frustrating when Grandmother can't find the right word to say. But you took the time to listen. I appreciate your patience and so does your grandmother." You can help too by modeling appropriate behavior and expressing your own feelings.

Take time for comfort and reassurance.

Most children are afraid of illness and may wonder if you will get Alzheimer's too. Increasing age and family history are the biggest known risk factors. However, physical and mental exercise, and maintaining healthy behaviors such as controlling blood pressure, weight, and cholesterol levels, may reduce your risk for Alzheimer's disease. You might say, "I know you are worried that I might get Alzheimer's disease. You need to know that I will take good care of myself and I'll be around for a long time."

Seek relief and respite care.

Parents may find themselves sandwiched between the caregiving needs of their parents and taking care of their children. With this added responsibility, it is important to find time for yourself and seek respite care as needed. Respite care allows caregivers to take a break while the person with Alzheimer's receives care from friends, family, or a professional, qualified caregiver. This respite time could be spent running errands, joining your child on a field trip, or doing something just for yourself.

Find your local Alzheimer's Association chapter.

The Alzheimer's Association has a national network of local chapters that provide reliable information and support to families and people with Alzheimer's disease. Chapters often have a telephone helpline, support groups, and lending libraries. Chapters also are a good source for finding community services such as respite or adult day care, assisted living or skilled nursing facilities, eldercare lawyers, or financial planners. To locate a chapter near you, call the Alzheimer's Association 24-hour helpline at (800) 272-3900 or visit www.alz.org.

ABOUT THE AUTHOR

Linda Scacco, Ph.D., is a licensed clinical psychologist who has worked with children and families. Currently Linda is an adjunct professor in the Psychology Department at the University of Hartford. After her uncle died with Alzheimer's disease in 1988, she wanted to write a book for children to help them understand and cope with the consequences of this devastating illness. Linda lives with her husband and three children in West Hartford, Connecticut.

ABOUT THE ILLUSTRATOR

Nicole Wong is a graduate of the Rhode Island School of Design. Her illustrations have been featured in several children's books, magazines, and greeting cards. Nicole lives with her husband and their dog and cat in Massachusetts.